SECRETS & LIES 6
By

H.M. WARD

LAREE BAILEY PRESS
www.HMWard.com

COPYRIGHT

LAREE BAILEY PRESS
First Edition: JUNE 2016
ISBN: 9781630351298

SECRETS & LIES 6

CHAPTER 1

I stand there flabbergasted, my jaw flapping in the wind. That can't be true. Josh raped someone? A heavy daze settles on my shoulders making the world around me morph into a fishbowl. Everything sounds far away and warped. My head is too heavy and I find myself reaching for a kitchen chair. I barely graze it with my fingertips and lower myself, not blinking, still shocked.

"Kerry, whoa, what are you—" Nate steps toward me, but it's too late.

It turns out said chair wasn't lined up with said ass. I pass the cute seat where my posterior should have landed on my way down to the linoleum floor. *Ooof.* I let out a hard rush of air on impact.

Nate rushes, offering a hand. "Are you okay?"

When I don't slip my palm into his, his crouch changes to a kneel. He places his hand on my shoulder. I want to cry or scream that Josh couldn't do something so heinous. There's no way. But he told me he did something horrible. I didn't believe him.

I glance over at the sexy professor's face. Nate is beautiful as always, but there are little worry lines around those cool blue eyes. The way he lingers close, waiting for me to respond—waiting to hear I'm all right—coupled with the confession of concern that lingers on his lips is way too intense. I didn't want a relationship. I can't handle another failure right now.

"Kerry?" Nate slides his knees around and sits on his back pockets, stretching those long legs out in front of him.

"Mmmm?"

"I know you care about this guy. I can tell from the way you're talking about him and the sucker-punched expression on your face."

I glance at him out of the corner of my eyes. "You're not jealous?" I'm a little shocked that the question fell out of my mouth, but yeah, it's weird. He's not pissing all over his territory like a horn-dog.

"It's not like that with us. You said so yourself. There's nothing lasting about this." He gestures between us. "As it is, it's insanely dicey for you to be here. Some things are worth the risk." Leaning in, he sweeps his lips against my cheek.

I stare straight forward and feel a rush of warmth flood through me. I'm in emotional overload. Fragments of my mind are cracking under duress and I no longer want to think about anything. That's what this guy is for—that's why I came here.

Nate's lips linger next to my cheek, a breath away. I turn slowly and lower my lashes, to watch his mouth. I stay there, not moving for a long time, lost in silence. When I finally lean forward to close the distance, my heart is pounding at a deafening volume and every inch of my skin tingles, anticipating Nate's touch.

Eyes fixated on his beautiful pink lips, I breathe, "Can you make me forget everything for a little while? I don't want to think anymore."

Nate answers by pressing his mouth to mine. At the same time, his hand laces around the back of my neck so he can pull me close. His other hand finds my cheek, and cups it as he kisses me harder. Thoughts scatter across my mind like a deck of cards in the wind. They're no longer in a neat stack, easily read and pondered. Instead, they're floating fragments that will soon be banished from my mind.

I concentrate on the way his mouth feels, on the touch of his tongue and the way he takes control of the kiss. I relax into him, letting him move me as he likes. A moment later, I feel my arm trembling and realize that I've leaned back and placed my hands behind me to prop my body up. I'm no longer able to support our weight, and before I can break the kiss to say so, Nate lowers me to the floor while keeping the kiss intact. His firm body comes down on top of mine, then shifts to the side while leaving one leg over my hips, knee bent, and pressing me to the floor. The coldness of the plastic tile against my back is jarring. I arch my back and gasp into his mouth as I tangle my hands in his hair.

Nate's lips soon drift from my mouth to my neck. There's not a thought in my head when his tongue touches that sensitive, smooth skin. Every time he kisses me there my eyes roll back and my lashes lower. I try not to moan, and then give up.

Nate smiles against my skin when I become vocal. He stops for a moment and pulls back enough to see my face. He's breathing hard and hovering right above me. He tucks a strand of hair behind my ear as he speaks. "Don't hide from me. Don't hold back. Pretend there's no tomorrow, no repercussions, no consequences."

Pressing my lips together nervously, I listen, wondering if I can do that—a little frightened of what it would mean. I will see him tomorrow. There will be consequences.

It's as if he can read my mind, because he adds, "This may be the last time we get to be together."

That punches my ticket. I understand what that means. No more Nate is like no more freedom, no more sweet, fresh air to fill my lungs and no freeing wind at my back. The world is listless and stale without him, and yet that's the way it is. We aren't supposed to be together. He's risking everything for this moment. His career will tank if someone discovers us. And my reputation will be torched. No one will believe I earned my grades—any of them. There will be sweeping assumptions that I screwed my way to the top, that I didn't deserve it. I know the risk and yet I can't walk away from him. I'm all too aware this could be the last chance we have to be together, and I don't want to hold back.

I slip my fingers around his neck and pull him down on top of me. I don't want him on the side. I want to be crushed to the floor. I want to feel his power, his strength. I want to be pinned in place and lose myself while he's inside me. If this is our last time, that's what I want. Clarity hits me hard and suddenly I'm all instinct and carnal urges. I'm writhing beneath him, spreading my legs wide, and bucking up into him wishing he'd free me from my jeans.

Breathless, I nip his neck as his hands rove my body. His hot mouth devours my neck as a lightness fills my body, making me smile. The bulge in his pants is hard and grinding against me, too many layers of fabric separating us. I don't want anything between us. I want to be covered in sweat and Nate. My stomach twists at the thought of being tangled together with Nate, skin on skin, slick and sweaty with him driving into me until I lose every inch of restraint and cry out his name.

I slam my hands into his chest, and flip us over. I straddle his lap with my thighs spread wide and shuck my shirt and bra in a blink. Then, I stand and kick off the rest of my clothes. When I straddle his hips again I'm completely naked. And he's not. He's still dressed with a nude woman on his lap.

A coy smile tugs at the corners of my lips as I sit there, watching his gaze consume every inch of me. When he lifts his hands, ready to touch the soft curves of my breasts, I stop him, threading my fingers through his and slamming them down next to his head.

"No touching."

Pinning his hands down with one to each side of his face, I lower myself so the curve of my breast is just above his lips. My nipples are taut and aching for his touch. I want him to take me in his mouth and tease me until I beg to be fucked.

Logic is trying to break through, but it's as soft as an echo. Is it so bad to want to be this man's plaything? The idea of being his fuckbuddy is immensely appealing, but I wonder if it's more than that. Is there more here? And do I want it if there is?

My thoughts suddenly rush away, caught in a current of lust as his lips come down around my nipple. He sucks me into his mouth tasting me, teasing me, and lavishing me with attention that makes it hard not to grind against him.

Moaning deeply, I pull him upright while staying on his lap, his mouth still on my breast. I gasp and throw my head back as he nips, sucks, and flicks my sensitive skin. Every inch of my body is hot and demands his touch. I want his hands on me, in me, and tangled in my hair. I want him to pull and tug, to own me and take me.

Nate rolls me back to the floor and continues his unrestrained affection, covering me with kisses. I'm vaguely aware that he kicks off his shoes, then I hear the sound of a zipper lowering, before he tugs my nip hard. Gasping, I dart upright slightly when he pulls away, watching him toss his shirt aside. He grabs a foil packet from his jeans and slips the condom in place. The beautiful naked man returns to me in an instant and presses me to the floor, crushing me against it. He spreads my thighs and skips the finger check. His hard length shoves inside me without caution. He's not shy about what he wants and I'm glad. I don't want to make love. I don't want gentle kindness and soft touches. I want to be fucked. I want to forget everything plaguing me and weighing me down. I want him to use me, to make himself feel totally high and take me with him.

As his hips pound against mine, his shaft slams harder with each thrust. I claw at his back and spread my legs wider, trying to take him deeper. I'm begging, asking him for things, telling him how much I want him as we slide across the kitchen floor—which doesn't have a crumb on it. I'm thinking of ordering take-out when we're done, eating down here, and making him fuck me again.

Mmm. Noodles.

The thought shatters when his lips touch my breast and he slams into me. The sensations are overwhelming and I start to buck uncontrollably, gasping for air, begging for release. It's too soon, but I don't care. I want him. I want him to come with me.

I cup his ass and grip his cheeks as he hammers into me until I can't control myself. I grab at him however I can, trying to force him harder, deeper, and bucking against him as the rhythm of our bodies gets frantic. I'm so close to the edge and have floated so high that I'm no longer aware of anything except him and me.

Crying out his name, I claw his waist as he presses into me. Heart pounding, I take him in deep and feel myself start to shatter. I can barely speak, but I manage to tell him, "Come with me."

Nate doesn't deny me. He pummels me harder as I shatter around him, crying out with ecstasy. Nate's body becomes rigid. He cries out at the same time, his voice deep and raw, with euphoria spreading across his face before he falls against my chest.

CHAPTER 2

Thinking I'm never going to be with Nate again changes things. I'm free to cut through the pretense that could have been there. The normal insecurities fade away and it's just us, two bodies, intertwined, moving in rhythm with one another. Pleasure lights me up, and after he gets up to take care of the condom, I stretch on the floor and stare at the ceiling. I've never been done on the kitchen floor before.

When Nate comes back, he's smiling, looking down at me. I'm a naked, sweaty, sated mess with my hands tucked behind my head and my ankles crossed. I tip my chin up at him, and coolly say, "'Sup?"

Nate laughs, and runs a hand over his head and then down his neck. When he smiles, those dimples show. God, he's beautiful. "Nothing much. Just had the most amazing, mind-blowing fuck of my life. How about you?" He stands next to me, one foot by my waist, the other by my shoulder.

I purr, "Mmmm, I'd have to agree."

"So, what now?" He places his hands on his hips and I'm treated to a delicious Superman pose.

Nate needs a cape. I make a mental note to buy him one. I'd love to fuck him with a cape on. Is that mental? Can I run to his linen closet, grab a sheet, and put it around his neck? Maybe grab a fan so the cape hem flutters in the breeze. Then I can lie back against the floor, gaze up at his package, and swoon inwardly. I can beg him to do me again. Or we can skip all that stuff and I can just say it.

"Do me."

"I just did." He smirks. "You can't possibly be ready for more."

I roll over onto my stomach, prop my head up in my hands and shrug. "Maybe."

Nate represses a cocky smile. "How do you want it, Kerry?"

I feel his eyes on my back and wonder what I want, how far I'm willing to go with him. There are some things I liked that Matt didn't, so we didn't do them. I want every memory of Matt gone, and the thought of Nate defiling me in every way possible is completely appealing.

I kick up my feet and cross my ankles as I lower my head to the floor and place it on my arms. I glance at him with a playful look. "How do you want to give it, Nate?"

He grins, straddles my hips, and then sits on my bare ass pinning me to the floor. He's facing toward my feet, but turns to the side, so I can see his profile. "Well, there's the obvious place, right here." I feel his finger touch my lower lips, slip inside, and push up into me. He turns toward me, watching my face from the corner of his eye as he does it. "I love fucking you here."

"Really?" I gasp, lips parted, teeth showing and try to hide how much I like his touch.

Nate's voice is light, happy. He watches me, eyes dark, as he slips his finger deeper before pulling his hand away. "Yes, it was a very pleasant experience, so much so that I'm thinking of leaving an online review. Five stars, your pussy is superior, perfect in every way."

I giggle. I can't help it. "Wow, you're going to Yelp! me? That's new."

"Well, I only write reviews when I'm floored. You're an amazingly good time. A good fuck, tight, wet, and all the things a guy could want, really."

Grinning, I look back at him. "Ugh! Not another review praising my pussy—that will make five this week! It's getting embarrassing." I tease him, flashing a bright smile his way.

"Right, the people." He refers to my comment a while back about doing it with randoms. "They like to ride Kerry."

"Damn straight." I shove my arm out to the side and offer a thumbs up.

He laughs. "I'm a jealous man, are you seriously going to taunt me with this?"

"Why not? It's not like you're going to do anything about it—" Before I can finish my sentence, he slips his hand between my legs and touches my clit, pressing it between his fingers, and then squeezes hard. I gasp and buck into the floor without meaning to. He laughs lightly and loosens his grip, but doesn't move his hand.

"What the hell?"

"What part of possessive don't you get? This is mine right now. Tomorrow is another story."

I'm still perplexed as to why my hips dry humped the floor when he touched me that way. Whatever he did made an involuntary response. I wonder if it was a fluke or if he can just do that. "That part is a little evasive. Can you explain it to me again?"

He repeats the touch, and the same thing happens. My legs spread wide and my hips buck, slamming down into the floor, but that's not the worst part. My body is on fire, begging to be fucked, suddenly a million times wetter and ever aware his dick is too far away. Desire becomes need and I think about him everywhere, filling me from every direction, all at once. It's like a flash of lust on crack. It comes and goes in a blink when he does that with his hand down there.

Breathless and gaping I look at his bare back, watch the lines of his muscles move as he breathes and wonder if he's really a sex god. He's incredibly beautiful and he can turn me into a total whore with minimal effort. The thing is, I was already thinking those thoughts they just weren't very loud. When he touched me like that, they became earsplittingly loud and writhing for attention.

He doesn't look back at me. "Tell me."

"Tell you what?" My voice comes out way too airy and an octave higher than usual.

He grins. "Tell me what you want most. What are your most carnal desires?"

I blush. There's no way I'm telling him I wish he had three dicks to fuck me with all at once. "Uh, I don't think so."

"Last chance, Kerry. We can do this the nice way or I can force it out of you."

"No you can't—" The rest of the sentence is suddenly sucked from my mind as if someone had placed a black hole in my brain. My thoughts are replaced with urges, things I need now. My breasts ache and I'm thinking things I can barely admit. But I want to do them. With him. Now.

He moves his hand, making me cry out loudly and tightening his grip on my sensitive flesh. My hips buck into the floor several times and I start saying insanely dirty things, begging him for it—telling him where I want him, how I'll take it any way I can just so long as he fucks me hard, now.

Nate speaks firmly, cutting into my dirty monologue, "I'm not letting you up until you tell me something."

I growl at him, as I try to clutch the floor, "Fuck me."

My hips slam down again and this time, I feel him—a finger slips inside—but it's not enough. I'm suddenly bucking so hard, backing into his hand, trying to fuck it. I'm not aware of anything else, and I feel my mind fighting my body for control and losing.

As I wildly pump against his finger, he asks, "What about here? Do you want me to fuck you here?"

While keeping his finger inside me, his thumb drifts south. It's what I was thinking and too shy to ask for. No woman in her right mind likes that, but I do. Right now I want him to fuck me every way he can.

My mind is screaming at me to shut up, my mouth is open and I'm begging him for things I thought I'd never say. The words will make my entire body turn red with a bright blush if I ever hear them again, but it doesn't stop me. I beg him and purr for him to do what I want.

Nate's voice is liquid sex, "That's the sluttiest thing I've ever heard."

His touch lit an intensity within me that I didn't know was there. Maybe it's because I just orgasmed or maybe it's because the last guy I was with didn't know his way around down there, but either way—I'm elated and terrified at the same time. Even so, I can't seem to shut up. I keep blurting out insanely sexy, carnal things—and demanding that he do them to me. Now.

Nate keeps his hand on me as he repositions himself behind me. I'm lying facedown on the kitchen floor.

Nate slaps my ass and demands, "Up." As I push up he hooks his arm under my hips and pulls me back to him. I slide across the floor and when I slam against him I feel how hard he is again.

He moves his hand away from me and grabs another condom. I'm wondering if I should be concerned that he has more than one on him.

Before I can think about it he puts it on and slips inside of me. My head is down, with my butt in the air. He slowly pushes in and then pulls out, watching as he does it. It's completely erotic and makes me think about sucking him off. I want to taste him in my mouth without protection. I want to feel his velvety skin instead of the plastic condom and taste his come as it drips down my throat. I want that with him—which makes me feel conflicted. If he's just a fuck there's no way I should do that. If he's more, we could. Do I want more?

I don't get a chance to ponder the question. He slams into me, and reaches around front, between my legs, and starts to do that motion again. I buck back into him and feel my heart pounding so hard that it might explode. I dart upright, so I'm kneeling and he's still inside of me. Weird position, but it feels good, putting pressure in all the right places.

Nate catches me with his other arm and holds me tight, restraining me. He whispers in my ear, "Don't move, Kerry. Stay like this for a moment." He's still and I feel his hot breath wash across my neck, and hear his quick gasps of air. "Do you like this? Being touched all over, being owned?"

I'm trembling as I try to stay still. I nod.

"Say it." He commands.

"No, I don't like it. I fucking love it." He moves his hand between my legs and pulls it away. The intensity of the carnal feelings flooding through me lessens, but they're still there, loudly demanding the same thing as before. The only difference now? My rational half can drown them out if I want.

He wraps his other arm around me, crushing me against his chest, gripping my breasts and holding me tight while his dick is barely inside of me, pressing in all the right places, making me totally nuts. I begin to arch my back to feel him deeper.

"Don't move," he says, scolding me. "Feel everything. Let it flood you. There's a damper on your sexuality. It's like it's muted or something. I'm guessing someone at some point told you something you wanted wasn't sexy and it made you shy away from it. I want all of you here with me. If you want a freaky fuck, I want to give it to you. Tell me what you want Kerry."

"I—" I'm trembling.

He's right. Matt did that. Losing it with him wasn't a thing. He wasn't the kind of guy that liked to think of himself as an animal with carnal needs. That pressure is gone, but the threat of disappointment still lingers. I know what I want, but I'm afraid to tell him.

A question pops up and I blurt it out. "How come that happens? I mean, touching me like that. It made me feel everything."

He breathes against my neck, his voice husky, "It's your sexual center. Touching it like that makes you light up like a sexy Christmas tree and every desire you have is suddenly clear. It makes your mind take a back seat."

"No one has ever touched me like that before."

"I think it's cheating, but you seem to be holding back. I won't do it again. I just wanted you to recognize what you wanted. I'll give it to you. Just say it, Kerry. Ask me for it." His top arm slides up so that is across the lower part of my throat, tipping my neck back. "Do you like this? It's a little too intense for some women."

I don't like him mentioning other women. I bristle. "It's a little lax for me. I want more. I want it rougher and mindless."

His lips are by my ear. He tightens his grip on my neck slightly, making my heart pound harder. "Tell me what's off limits with you. I'll give you everything you want, but I need to know if there's something you don't want to do."

I turn my face to glance over my shoulder. I want to see his eyes. When his blue gaze locks with mine, I confess, "I want this. I like it intense. I like it when you touch me like that, and make me mindless. And to be clear, I'm okay with anything, anywhere. And I'd really like you to lose the condom."

He's perfectly still and for a second I think I've freaked him out. I keep thinking about how much better this will be without the sheath, and how much more we'll feel without it. "You trust me that much?"

"I do."

Nate pulls out of me, spins me around, so we're face to face. "Kerry, are you sure? That makes things a lot more intimate."

"I've already told you how I want to be taken and said things I'll deny when I see you again. This never happened. I wasn't here." I splay my hands on his chest and look up into his eyes. "I want everything. I don't want to wonder. I'm on the pill and have been for a while. I don't have anything contagious or concerning—no STDs or weird infections. Do you?"

"No." His gaze is brilliantly blue and wide, completely focused on me. His lips part slightly as he waits for my reply, perched like he's incredibly excited or worried.

It's funny how those two things can look the same at times. It's the moment before you decide to literally jump off the cliff. It takes guts and a good amount of stupidity to actually consider doing it, but the amount of determination and courage needed to put said plan into action—to actually drag your feet toward the edge and hurl your body out into space—that's something altogether different.

There's a bit of doubt that continues to echo through my mind. It skittered in the day Matt dumped me and has been gnawing at me ever since. It's like my mind is infested with doubt. All the what-ifs and failed attempts to become who I wanted to be won't shut up. I thought I'd have the great love story. I found the boy when we were kids and we'd be together forever. Picket fences and 2.5 kids later, I'd be a schoolteacher and stay home during the summer to tend our little piece of the American dream.

But when Matt broke things off with me, that dream shattered. A wild weed grew up in the chasm he left in my heart, sinking its roots deep and making me pause, its bloom alluring and deadly. It taunts me with every impulse I've ever had and was too afraid to follow. It whispers of chances untaken and breathless encounters yet to be explored. It's freeing and scary. It lifts me up and takes me high—so high I'm afraid the fall alone will kill me. I'm averse to taking risks and pushing the envelope, but that wild part of me— the part I didn't know was there until recently— I'm having trouble tuning it out. The problem is daunting and I haven't a clue as to how to fix it.

How am I supposed to silence a part of me that's crying out for freedom? Because that's what it sounds like—a shrill voice in the darkness refusing to shrivel up and die. Is that really who I am? Is that wildness me? How am I supposed to know?

The thoughts rush through my mind in a cascade, flowing so rapidly I can't possibly set my finger on one thought. Instead they merge and rush through me, cold and pressing, pushing me forward and filling my body with a cool confidence that's completely intoxicating. I'm power-drunk and I love it. At this moment, Nate is enthralled and I'm the woman who's got him on a hook. He wants anything I offer, and isn't holding anything back, so why should I?

I call it. Cautious Kerry is dead. This is the new me. I surveyed the cliff and stared into the sun. The blinding light beckons to me, calling me forward. The rush of lust and adrenaline mingle and my shoulders pull back as my chest curves out into a classic S-curve.

Posed naked in front of him, I say with a flirtatious smile on my lips, "I'm game for anything and everything. Ditching the condom is your call. Do your best. Leave me so breathless I forget my name."

Nate suppresses a grin as he steps back and pulls off the condom.

CHAPTER 3

Sated, with a silly grin on my face, I lie in Nate's bed for a while. We say nothing and I wonder if he regrets anything. I'm not asking because I sure as hell don't, which surprises me. I did things with him that I've never done before, acts that will make my cheeks burn in the light of day. He had me so wildly turned on that I didn't think at all. I was a basic version of myself— Kerry 1.0. Apparently, she doesn't say much and fucks hard. She also likes orange juice in copious amounts. I've already had three glasses and decide to go finish off the carton.

When I swing my legs out of bed and my feet hit the floor, I would normally stop and pull on a shirt or something to cover up my nakedness. The curve of my stomach is too big and the padding on my hips shows how much I like milkshakes. I'm not Amazon Barbie, but I feel okay with myself at the moment, so I bypass the clothing and pad down the hallway nude. I feel Nate's eyes on me appreciating the view as I head to the kitchen.

I call back to him, "Can I get you anything?"

"Water would be great." His voice is gravelly, rough from voicing deep commands. Combined with that throaty groans of pleasure that erupted when I did certain things, things that make me go hot now that I think about them, it's no wonder his voice sounds rough.

"You got it."

I don't bother turning on the lights in the kitchen. I've been in here a few times already and have an idea where things are, well the things that matter anyway. Nate's fridge was nearly bare when I got here, and now it's totally empty. The guy hates grocery shopping, so he only had a few odds and ends that came from a convenience store down the block. I might have to stop there next time I head over here for another fuckfest. Assuming there is another.

I pause and consider not being with him again. That would suck. He's been good for me, despite our rough start. I hope I've been good for him. Based on the way he spoke my name earlier, I know at the very least that he had a good time.

As I stare into the fridge, I fixate on the tiny light at the back of the icebox. It illuminates the small kitchen, casting shadows into the dark corners. I grab the carton, crack the top, and tip it back, guzzling the OJ. My throat hurts—a particular sexy act didn't go according to plan—and the cool liquid feels good.

When I come up for air, I call back to Nate, "I think I bruised my uvula."

His laughter reaches me and he says something, but I don't hear him.

Something in the dark corner catches my eye in my peripheral, and I turn slowly. The hairs on my arms stand on end and my heart thumps wildly. Someone is watching me. I feel eyes on me. As I turn and look at the empty table and chairs, I scan the room. There's no one here. I pad across the linoleum and toward the back door. The darkness hid it before, but I see it now. There's a space, a dim crack of light between the jamb and the door—it's open. Someone was here.

Stepping forward, I put my palm on the door and push it shut, and lock it. As I do so, a small slip of paper protrudes from the slit in the door.

I pull it out and scan the scribble:

PAY YOUR DEBT AT NINE
SUNDAY NIGHT

My heart sinks as I stare at the note. It's from Ferro. It has to be. I crumple up the paper and try to push aside the bile that rises up in my mouth. He was here, in the house? Did he watch us? That's disgusting! Even worse, how did I not notice him? Couldn't I tell if someone were here? Caution was the furthest thing from my mind at the time. I was secure in thinking Nate and I were the only ones in the house. Although, I doubt I'd be aware of anything but Nate, wrapped up in him the way I was.

I guzzle the rest of the juice and stuff the note in the carton before tossing it in the trash. Worry pinches my face and that uneasy sensation settles once more into the pit of my stomach. I grab Nate a glass from the cabinet and fill it with water. As I pad back to his room, I decide I need to tell him what I did to get this house back before it blows up in my face. I just have to find the right time.

CHAPTER 4

The right moment doesn't present itself quickly. Nothing is effortless when it comes to me. Why did I think telling Nate I nearly castrated his biological father to get back his house would be easy? It's nearly four in the morning by the time I roll out of his bed. Nate's dark lashes flutter as he attempts to keep his gaze locked on my face, but sleep paws at him until he succumbs.

Quietly, I slip on my clothes without waking him. I hate goodbyes. Besides, what am I supposed to say to the guy? Thanks for blowing my mind and giving me more orgasms in one day than I've had in my entire life…by the way, I drank all your juice. Yeah, no thanks.

As I sneak out the front door and pull it closed, I feel like a douche. Not saying goodbye is lame, but I don't want to wake him and I can't stay until sunrise. As it is, the bus is a sore thumb and my stupid, oversized rodent also came out for a booty call last night. He doesn't exactly operate in stealth mode. While I was having a good time, he went at it too. The little bastard made love to all the trashcans on the block.

As I stand at the curb in rumpled clothes and serious sex hair, I gape. There's not one garbage pail left standing. They all lie on their sides with the contents strewn all over the asphalt.

"Crap," I mutter to myself, wondering if I should pick them all up. It'd take the rest of the night. That little rat tipped every single can, save one.

I turn and gaze at Nate's trash in the brown pail, neatly waiting at the curb for removal. That's bad for business. All his neighbors are going to think that Nate's weird friend with the bus went through their trash.

As if on cue, the fuzzy little pain in the ass comes waddling toward me before curving to make a beeline for the bus. I whisper-rant at him, "You had to eat everyone's garbage, didn't you? Jeez, PITA!" I shake my head and put fists on my hips, glaring at him. The raccoon doesn't respond. He's such a bitch. "That's your name now, pain in the ass. I hope you're happy."

So I do what any other girl in my situation would do. I head to the curb and glance up and down the block, making sure I'm unobserved before taking Nate's trashcan and knocking it over. The lid falls off and white GLAD bags fall out. The neighbor's dumped pails are messier.

Holy hell, I can't believe I'm doing this. I bend over and grab the plastic, ripping it with my nails and then kicking the bag so the garbage spills out. An empty KFC container and chicken bones goes flying along with tissues and a ridiculous amount of dental floss. Nate has a flossing fetish and seriously needs an intervention, because what the hell? I stare at the ball of blue floss, tangled in the chicken carcass. I don't have time to ponder my lover's dental obsession. I need to make his garbage as messy as everyone else's, so I repeat the slash and trash to two more bags and then hightail it to my bus.

When I climb the stairs, the little beast hisses at me, like I went to a party without him. As I start the engine, I snap at him, "Oh shut up, Pita. It's not like I could clean it all up. What else was I supposed to do?"

Of course, if Nate knew I ripped up his garbage, he might have second thoughts about banging me again. Don't dip your wick in crazy is a dude mantra and playing in his garbage is a few ticks past insane. It's the equivalent of eating my freak flag with ketchup. At the same time, floss much, Nate?

Pita hisses and then scratches the leather seat and settles in as the bus lurches to life. I get the hell out of there, and don't look back.

CHAPTER 5

The next day I'm a zombie. I plop down hard at the lunch table across from Emily. She's sporting a freshly dyed head of Kool-Aid colored blue and grape hair. The spiked dog collar has been replaced with a strap that looks like it came from a bra.

I stare at it. "New choker?"

She lifts a pierced brow and nods. "Upcycled."

"As in it went higher than your tits?" I say it straight-faced and stuff a taco in my mouth.

Emily nearly chokes on her soda. Her jaw drops and she looks me over. "No, upcycled—as in recycled with a higher, more glam purpose. That was slightly ostentatious for this time of day. What got into you?" Her gaze slips over me, appraisingly, and then the corner of her mouth tips up and I get treated to a nod of respect.

"Nothing. I'm just sick of pussyfooting around all the time. I'm going to be blunt for the rest of my life. You have a bra strap on your neck, dude. Phys Ed sweats make up ninety percent of my wardrobe. We both are freaked out by those stairs at the bar."

Emily snorts, "With good reason."

I munch another bite and wipe a piece of lettuce off my lip before saying, mouth still full, "I like the strap choker. It's like a big 'F YOU' to everyone. The hair rocks, too."

Emily preens and her shoulders go back, neck long and lean. You'd think I paid her the highest compliment she ever received. Apparently, she was going for the 'fuck off' outfit and nailed it. "You don't look so bad yourself. I like the new non-gym attire. It's like you're not a PE major or something. Once you get a few paint stains on those jeans, you'll blend right in with the rest of us."

I laugh and wince slightly, careful not to put my hand on my distressed muscles. My all-nighter made it very clear I don't have abs of steel. "I'm sure."

Emily notices how I tense I am and the way my eyes start to press shut. Chewing her food in the side of her mouth, she swallows and asks, "Working out?"

You could say that. "Yeah. I'm channeling all my unresolved anger into an awesome workout plan."

Also known as the 'screw Nate until I can't walk' method. It's done wonders for my mood. I feel light and limber. The part of me that was emotionally overridden and shorting out has stopped arcing like a fork in a microwave. I was totally ready to blow, well, not like that. Although, that was a good diversion. Nate tastes good, sweet almost. Probably from drinking all that juice. I smirk, not meaning to. I need to buy him some more OJ.

Emily's fork balances on her finger as she stares at me. "A new workout plan? Is it hard?"

I suppress a grin. "Yeah, it's really hard, the hardest I've ever done." Double entendre. Inner giggle. I go straight-faced when Emily blinks at me, not looking away.

"Does it target your stomach and butt?"

"Amongst other areas, yeah." I'm stuffing a taco in my face to hide my I-had-sex smile.

Emily nods. At first I don't think she has a clue. She keeps stepping in it, rambling on about how she needs to work on her ass and if this new exercise could make her tighter, perkier.

"Totally, all of the above." Tighter, perkier, and all around happier.

Carter saunters over with a tray in his hands and sits down next to me. A rail of a guy who is uber tall and covered in piercings, also sits down next to Emily and suddenly there are a lot of people.

The conversation keeps going and Carter chimes in. "You hit 25,000 steps yesterday. What the hell were you doing?" Carter pulls the tomatoes off his tacos as he watches me out of the corner of his eyes.

The Fitbit. Damn it. I forgot to take it off last night. Emily says casually, "New workout. She was at it all night."

"Yeah." I stuff a taco in my face and wish I had more food to hide behind. I need to get out of here before he starts asking questions. As it is, I think Emily knows.

She flashes a cool look my way and continues, "Next time you work out, bring me with you." It's a command, not open for rejection.

I hedge, "It's not really a group thing."

Her eyes flash and my stomach sinks. She knows. She has to know, but if she did then she'd be in my face about Nate being a professor. She'd hate me. Maybe she hasn't figured it out after all. "Since when is an exercise class not a group thing?"

"Well, I meant they don't have any more openings." I start collecting my tray, throwing my utensils on top of my plate, and slip my fingers under the tray preparing to stand. "I need to run."

"Where's it at?" Emily presses.

I'm standing now and about to walk away from the table. "I don't have the address. I'll grab it for you later, okay?"

Carter picks up his phone and speaks while his eyes are glued to the screen. "I can grab the address for you. Kerry, just open the—" his voice trails off as he pushes buttons on the screen.

"I said I'll get it later. Carter, stop—" But he doesn't. I know what he's going to see before he opens it.

The Fitbit has GPS.

It's normally used to show which running path the wearer took and clocks miles when there's vigorous movement. Carter set up the Fitbit so it would share everything with him. It was supposed to be for fun, to see who could take more steps. At least that's what he said when he put the app on my phone and added me as his friend in the app. He'll see everything. It'll pinpoint Nate's house and show wiggly purple lines all over his property. How the hell am I supposed to explain that?

Maybe he won't know it's Nate's house. Maybe I can lie and say I was running on a treadmill for hours. That sounds plausible, assuming he's never been to Nate's house. Some teachers invite students over to their homes, usually at the end of the semester. I haven't been here long enough to know if Nate is one of those types of professors.

Carter's features turn stoic. Shit. He knows. His gaze lingers on the screen like he recognizes that address. His expression is lost in the middle, somewhere between regret and shock. The corners of his mouth turn up and he sports a plastic smile. "Oh yeah, that place. It's the fitness center on the corner of Amarillo with all the new equipment."

I stand there, stunned that he covers for me.

"Yeah, they're open 24 hours." I add to the lie, not thinking. I want Carter to face me, to say that he doesn't blame me for seeing Nate. But that's not the way it goes. Instead of anger, I get apathy. Surprisingly, it feels much worse.

Emily starts talking to the other guy and their conversation shifts toward other things. I linger with my tray in my hands, and then say softly, "Carter?"

"Yeah?" He doesn't turn. He acts unaffected, continuing to shovel his lunch in his mouth.

"Can you walk with me? I wanted to ask you about something." The pit of my stomach twists and the tacos aren't sitting well.

"Yeah." He grabs his tray and hauls ass across the cafeteria, dumping his tray of half-eaten food before exiting.

I follow him into the student center, and then outside into the quad. We walk along the bricked path for a while before I finally spit it out. "Why did you cover for me?"

He shrugs. Says nothing.

"Carter, I met him before I knew he was teaching here."

"And you should have stopped when you realized there was a serious conflict of interest." He turns toward me, stopping, his face flashing with alternating blasts of anger and disappointment.

"Weeks had passed by then. I thought he was a teaching assistant and he thought I was a model. He didn't know what Dr. Jax did the first week of class—how I ended up modeling. Anyway, that's over now. I'm not doing it anymore. Things can go back to the way they were." I reach for his arm, but he glares at me. I drop my hand.

"Right, because that makes screwing the teacher more acceptable. It doesn't affect your grades at all." His voice is high as he hurls barbs at me, his hands flying through the air as he rants. "There's no way he'd favor you after something like that. No man can compartmentalize that much, Kerry. If you want to whore your way to an early graduation, go ahead. Who am I to judge?"

Something inside me snaps. Nate's the only shred of peace I've had since I stepped foot in this state, and there's no way in Hell I'm going to let Carter piss on it. I plaster both palms on his chest and shove. "Hey! How dare you say that to me? I told you what happened and with everything else going on in my life—"

He cuts me off, "Oh, boo hoo. Suck it up, Kerry. Everyone has shit going on. You're not the only one whose life got fucked up. You can't blame other people for your problems and you sure as hell can't cheat your way through college, not while I'm still breathing."

I blanch. "Are you threatening me?"

"It's not a threat. Break it off with Professor Smith or I'll go straight to administration. He'll be fired and you'll get expelled." Carter's face is stone, completely devoid of emotion.

It feels like he's reached into my chest and ripped out my lungs. I can't breathe. "Carter, it's not like that. We don't have a relationship. We're not dating."

He rolls his eyes and laughs bitterly. "Got it. I was right the first time and it's whoring around, is it?"

"No, you stupid, thoughtless ass! It's my life and I don't have to justify my actions to you!" I'm in his face, yelling. My hands fist at my sides and I don't know where to put them. I want to strangle him, hit him, and make him be my friend again. Where did my Carter go? It's like he was never there at all.

He clucks his tongue and shakes his head. He places his hand on my shoulder and steps in closer before saying softly, "That's where you're wrong. You have to make me believe you've earned every grade given to you by Nathan Smith without an ounce of doubt. If you don't convince me, you'll end up back where you started with your idiot mother and your ex-boyfriend who prefers the older sagging Kerry Hill model."

Fire surges through my veins and propels my fist to draw back, and then fly forward. All the pain and fear of my mother's affair is packed into that punch. Every ounce of betrayal, every last bit of doubt and self-loathing laces around each finger, making my fist stronger, urging my arm onward and pulling the weight of my body behind it.

When my knuckles connect with his jaw, Carter's head swings to the side. Everything happens in seconds, but the movements inch by slowly as if suspended in time. As my fist drops, his eyes slide to meet mine.

Shock and hurt are apparent, but then his gaze becomes dull, lifeless. Carter acts like nothing happened. He straightens and looks down at me. "Like I said, if I see you at his house again, I'm reporting it. And keep the Fitbit on, Kerry, or I'll head to the dean's office right now."

As I watch him walk away, anger gushes through me, but something milder is tempering it and keeping me from following him. I don't know if it's disappointment or the fact that I'm certain I've lost another friend, but it douses my rage until it's barely an ember.

CHAPTER 6

I'm standing on the sidewalk, alone, when Josh passes by. I watch him, but don't move. We don't walk toward each other or wave. There's no laughter on his face today and all the mirth has been sucked from my soul at the moment. My arms are wrapped around my middle and I'm feeling small, wishing I didn't have such shitty relationships. Every single friendship is tainted with something bad, something I can't quite navigate.

Josh stops and stands there. It's like he wants to come over, but won't be the first one to step forward. I sigh, drop my arms, and walk toward him. When I'm close enough, he asks, "Are you all right?"

Nodding, I answer, "Yeah, I'm fine. I take it you saw that whole mess?"

"Unfortunately. I'm sorry, Kerry."

"Yeah, well, don't be. He's not worth it. You were right all along."

Josh hesitates and then asks, "Did you do what I asked? Do you know about me, about what I did?" His lips thin as he presses them tightly and stuffs his hands in his pockets. His gaze shifts so that it's clear he doesn't want to look me in the eye at the moment.

"I don't believe it. There had to be a reason, or a misunderstanding, right?" My voice raises an octave and comes out like a whisper. "I just can't believe you raped a girl."

Josh's face twists into disgust. "Are you serious? Even after reading all that, you think there's no way I did it? Kerry, I did it—"

Shaking my head, I step back. "It's not possible. You're too—"

"You're not listening. There was no mistake, no misunderstanding. There was nothing to misunderstand." His green eyes bore into me as his lips curl in disgust. "How could you even think?" He pauses and then a moment later, adds, "You didn't read the report. Someone told you and you didn't bother reading anything about it."

"No, I didn't read anything. There's no way that you did something like that. You're not that kind of guy." Before I can finish my thoughts, Josh pulls out his phone, navigates to an article and hands it to me.

"This is the truth and it's something you need to know if you care about me in any way, shape, or form. Read it."

My heart rises up into my throat and thumps there for a moment. I can't swallow it back down, and I don't want to see what he's showing me. I take his phone and look down at a police report. An intoxicated Joshua Gallub sexually assaulted a co-ed at a party on Halloween his freshman year. There are pictures, a torn Cleopatra costume, bruises on her thighs and wrists. My lower lip trembles as I read in graphic detail the events of that night and what he did to that woman.

When I finish, I'm shaking, unable to hide it. Tears sting my eyes, but don't fall. There's only one word in my mind, one relentless question that won't be still. "Why?"

His eyes avoid mine as he turns from me, and stares at a point on the horizon. "There was no reason. I did it. I wanted her, and when she said no, I didn't stop. I lost everything important to me that night, but she lost so much more. I was horrified the next day when I realized what I did. I went to find her, to apologize, but there's no way to make amends for something like that. Kerry, I killed part of her. She'll never be the same because of me. No matter what I do, I can't fix that."

"What happened?"

"She reported it to the campus police that night and they blew her off."

"What?"

"They didn't believe her. She was dancing with me that night, and a lot of people saw us making out. They blamed her, said she must have sent mixed signals to a drunk guy and that she needed to get her story straight before she comes in crying wolf."

"Oh my god. What happened? How did the police hear about this, then?"

He looks up at me. "I told them."

"What?" I stare at his face, dually shocked. "You reported it?"

"There's no way to fix it, but I didn't want her thinking that it was her fault. It wasn't. I reported it. There was no trial, no questioning. I put her through enough. I had my lawyer ask her what she wanted, how I should pay for what I did. She asked for leniency in exchange for a promise. I had to give my word that I would tell every woman who I had any interest in about that night. I agreed and kept my promise."

No wonder why he's a pariah. It's something no one talks about, but Josh is isolated most of the time. "Was this Carter's girlfriend?"

"Yes." He says the word looking directly into my eyes. "People say I stole her, that we dated for a while. We didn't. That's just a nicer story to hear. Carter never forgave me, and I can't blame him."

"And the gay jibes at Carter? He said you started that."

"I didn't start it, but I didn't stop it either. I may have added to it and made sure it stuck." He sighs deeply. "Kerry, I fucked up. I ruined someone. I broke her." Remorse fills his features and he continues, "I like you a lot, but I don't trust myself anymore and you shouldn't trust me either."

I nod, finally understanding the pain in his eyes. Grief never released him and there's no penance that can make up for what he did. I don't know if I'm disgusted, disappointed, or just drained, but I want to cry. Josh wasn't supposed to be the bad guy. I hand him back his phone and stare into space, not knowing what to say.

"You don't have to pretend with me, Kerry. I was a bad person. Now, I don't know what I am, but I don't deserve your compassion."

"Did you go to jail?"

"I can't talk about it beyond what I've said. It was part of the agreement."

I blink at him. "You don't trust yourself anymore, with anything, do you?"

"No."

I want to punch him and hug him. I want to scream and weep. How could he do something so despicable? "I don't know what to say."

"There's nothing to say." We stand there for a moment in an uncomfortable silence. Josh turns away and leaves without another word.

CHAPTER 7

The rest of the week crawls by at slug speed. College was supposed to be this glorious chance to start over, to be the woman I always wanted to become. The problems that flared up around me like little evil infernos prevent me from seeing that far ahead. I've been in survival mode the entire time I've been here, patching things up with tape instead of actually repairing anything the right way. That would have taken too much time, and that's a luxury that I don't possess. My life is covered in Band-Aids at the moment and there's no reprieve in sight. At least I have Beth. She's been a true friend when everyone else disappointed.

Beth strides next to me as we walk across campus. The sky is inky and littered with stars.

It's late Saturday night and we're both wearing ankle length full skirts with floral prints. Beth gave me mine as a present and I'm surprised how much I like it. I figured I'd trip over the hem, but so far there's no problem. Coupled with a t-shirt and flip-flops, I feel cool, confident, and pretty, which is a nice combination.

I've wanted to talk to Beth about my meeting with Ferro tomorrow and get her caught up on Carter. I have no idea how to talk to her about Josh, so I don't. I have to finish a painting I've been working on all semester and we were given access to the building on weekends in order to complete the assignment. I pull out my ID card, swipe it through the card reader, yank open the glass door, letting Beth pass through.

She glances over her shoulder, speaking as she walks. "I can't imagine what he wants to ask you to do. The guy thinks you're a criminal."

I step in behind her and make sure the door closes and latches shut behind me. I don't like being in the dark halls by myself at night. The building creaks and makes freaky sounds. "Not anymore. If he didn't look me up as soon as I left, I'd die of shock."

As we make our way up the staircase and down the darkened halls, there is amber light spilling beneath Nate's office door as we pass by. Is he still here? I glance at my Fitbit to check the time, still wearing it because I'm worried about Carter ratting me out. It's after ten. Why is Nate still here? I haven't seen him outside of class after the night we were together. Since then he's acted distant, detached. It irks me if I think about it too long, so I don't think about it at all.

"Hottie is here, huh?" Beth tips her head toward the door as we walk by, her long skirt billowing around her ankles.

"Apparently."

"Maybe he's waiting for a booty call." She smirks. When she sees the look on my face her smile falls. "What's wrong?"

After we're in the classroom, I flick the lights on and close the door. When I'm sure no one else is there, I confide in her, finally telling her what happened with Carter. "He's tracking me with this. I can't take it off or he'll tell the dean and then I'm toast. Everything I worked for, all the respect I earned will be gone. If anything, Nate has been grading me harder to compensate for things. That's the only class where I didn't pull straight A's. Beth, I don't know what to do."

Beth's small face pinches together as she listens. "What an asshole."

"Carter isn't who I thought he was."

"I'm sorry. I know how much that has to sting right now."

"It does, but I don't want him to lose it and say something. I'm the one who pissed him off, and I don't want to take Nate down with me."

"So there's only one thing to do. Stop seeing Nate."

I pull out my canvas as we are talking and put it on the easel. Then I grab my pallet, brushes, and paint and start mixing my colors. As I blend the right hues, I say, "I have, but there's no promise Carter won't say anything. He was really mad. He thinks I cheated."

"Cheated with what?" Beth sits on the floor and leans back against a cabinet.

"I'm in upper level classes. It's unusual."

"Uhm, did he look at your work? It's not like you're drawing stick men, Kerry. You're good at this." She gestures to my painting. "I really like that. It's different."

"Thanks." I step back, and examine my work before taking a brush to it again. It's a dark piece made of swirling lines. A young girl wears a white shift. Her back is to us, and she's standing in a garden facing an open gate that leads into darkness. I didn't plan this piece. It just happened. I wonder how much of this reflects my life and cringe at making my thoughts so visible.

"What else do you need to do to it? It looks finished to me."

I stand there, staring at it. "I wish I knew, but it's not done. There's something missing."

The highlights and shadows are well distributed. The focal point is clear. The flow of the piece allows the eye to enter, rest on the focal point, and move through the work easily. It's not an issue with the composition or the color, but something about it is lacking.

As I stand there and think, I tweak some highlights and shadows, but it doesn't finish the piece. Beth and I talk for over an hour and eventually she pushes up off the floor. "I need to head back. Josh will have a fit if I'm not at the house tonight and I still need to crank out a paper before morning."

I have no idea how she does it. Beth is the world's worst procrastinator. She waits until the last possible second to write her papers, but manages to hand them in on time and keeps good grades.

"How is he?" I ask carefully.

Beth notices, walks over, and steps up next to me. "He's been out of sorts for the past few days."

"He told me about something." I stand there, gaping at the paint, horrified that I said those words. I wasn't going to tell her. I'm sure she knows everything about Josh.

Beth's eyes are on the side of my face. "He told you." It's a statement, murmured quietly, unbelievingly. "Seriously? You couldn't stay away from him?" Her face crumples and she shakes her head, backing away from me, scolding, "You're nailing Nate and that's not enough, you have to get with Josh, too?" Disgusted, Beth rushes away from me, throws open the classroom door, and takes off down the hall.

What just happened? Why did she behave like that? "Hey, wait a second!" I drop my brushes and rush after her, not catching up until we're in the dark hallway. I grab her elbow and whirl her around. "I didn't do anything. Beth, he just told me."

Her eyes are glassy. "Right, because he likes you. And the one thing I asked was that you guys didn't get together, because when it falls apart—"

"We're not together. Beth, it's not like that."

"Did you kiss him?" She presses, pointblank. "Well?" When I don't answer, her eyes cut to the side and she lets out a rush of air. "I've done this before and I'm not doing it again." She turns on her Chinese slippered heel and stomps off down the hall, pissed.

"I'm sorry. It wasn't supposed to end up like this." I call after her, apologizing, but she doesn't answer, and doesn't stop.

There were several reasons why I shouldn't have kissed Josh, but this is the main one—Beth. She said no, and I didn't listen.

CHAPTER 8

I head back into the classroom and start cleaning up. I screw the tops back on my paint tubes and head over to the sink to clean my brushes. As I stand there, rubbing my thumb over the fine hairs and watching a ribbon of colors run down the drain, I stare. The water softens the colors, blends them from one muted hue to another, tangling the colors, but keeping them separate. I lift my gaze across the room to my painting, and then back down to the brush. It's that soft harmony that catches my attention and makes me wonder. I want to capture the opposite. I want movement and anguish. I suddenly see what I need to do, but I'm not sure if I have the guts to do it. If I'm wrong it will mess up the whole painting and I won't be able to fix it.

I twist off the faucet and take the clean brush over to my canvas. The paint is piled on thickly, creating texture and depth. If I turn my brush around and scrape into the wet paint it could be everything I wanted. I can't hesitate. I have to do it with confidence or it'll show. There can't be wiggly lines here. They need to be curved, drawn fast and hard.

Sucking in air, I stay my hand, bite my lip, and slash at the canvas with the wrong end of the paintbrush. I do it again and again, marking the work over and over, leaving no section untouched. The smooth surface is marred by gouges that cut all the way down to the canvas, leaving a pale streak of color in its wake across the fine weave of the fabric.

I have no idea how much time has passed. I've been slashing at it, filling the sky with swirls and her dress with little gashes, and flaying her hair until the entire canvas is covered in gouges.

I don't hear him enter the room. The sound of the door opening never caught my attention. I'm so wrapped up in what I'm doing that I don't notice Nate until he's standing next to me. A dusting of dark stubble lines his jaw. His Oxford shirt is unbuttoned at the neck, cuffs rolled up, and pushed back over the thick muscles of his forearms. The hem of his shirt is untucked and he shucked his tie hours ago. He folds his arms over his chest and spreads his jean-clad ankles a shoulder width apart, surveying my painting with me.

For a while he says nothing, and then nods slowly like he appreciates what he sees. "This was brave. Did it have the desired effect?"

I'm still staring at the painting with my arms at my sides. "I think so."

"Movement, anarchy, fear, wanting, and so much more is conveyed in this piece now. It wasn't there before."

I agree with him. "No, it wasn't."

Nate's eyes are glued to the canvas, slipping over it, drinking it in. "It's as if you added air to this piece. There's breath and life in the girl, wind in the sky which gusts against the grass and foliage. At the same time the pattern makes it feel like there's never enough oxygen. I can't tell which way she's going to run, but it's clear she has to run."

I turn and look at him. There are dark circles under his eyes like he hasn't slept for days. "What's wrong?"

Nate finally looks down at me, unfolds his arms, and then runs a hand through his hair. His beautiful face is weary, and the corners of his eyes are pinched with worry. "Nothing, just a long few days." He inhales deeply and lets out a tired sigh.

My hair is in a ponytail with extra paintbrushes sticking out from the back of my head like a spiky crown. "Yeah, it's been a long week."

I feel his eyes on me, sliding down my face to my neck, and then dipping further before coming back up. He steps closer to me and breathes in my ear, "Do you want to talk?"

"No," I say flatly. He hasn't been around and everything is falling apart. I'm falling apart. I want to cry on his shoulder and tell him what's wrong, but that's off limits. There's no relationship here, nothing like that can transpire between us. And with Carter's threat looming, I should walk away. This conversation should stop right now.

Nate steps closer and his lips brush my cheek when he speaks, making my skin tingle. "Can I help you with anything?"

My eyes close as the pretend kiss sweeps over my skin. I want to fall into him and melt. I want to forget about everything else and just be his for a while. But I can't do that either. Carter will know. I stare at the stupid device on my wrist and wish I could take it off.

"No." I force out the word.

Nate remains where he is, too close, his breath tickling my neck in a delicious way that makes my insides warm and uncurl. "Let me rephrase, can I help you forget something, Miss Hill?"

The way he says my name, the sexy deepness of his voice is hypnotic. He doesn't touch me, but he's close enough that my entire body is on edge at his closeness. I feel him there, inches away, and want more. I want his hands on my skin and his lips on my body. I want to get lost in his kisses and be devoured the way he did last time. I want to scream out as I find my release and dig my nails into his skin, marking him, making him mine.

But he's not mine.

And this can't be.

I force myself to step away. The seduction spell falters, but doesn't dissipate entirely. It never does when Nate's in the room. I head to the sink and turn on the water. "Not tonight, but thanks for the offer."

Nate remains by my painting across the room. He watches me at the sink, and notices how I avoid his gaze. "Did I do something wrong?"

"No, everything is fine."

"Kerry—"

I don't want him to know about Carter, about the threats. I can handle it and if we stay apart, it won't matter. The whole mess is over if I can keep my hands to myself.

"Nate, I'm fine." I smile at him and pass by, playfully bumping my shoulder to his as I pass. "It's just late and I have to be up early tomorrow."

Nate folds his arms across his chest and eyes me as I finish cleaning up my paints. "You seem upset."

"I'm not." I flash a super big fake smile his way. "See? I'm good."

He walks up behind me and places his hand over mine. "I know you're not fine. You were rattled last time we talked, and now it seems worse. If you need help, you can ask me. For anything, Kerry—not just sex."

The words are exactly what I want to hear, but I can't accept them. I twist around and I'm between my easel and Nate, with little room to do anything. Wet paint is behind me and a very hot man is in front of me, saying magical words that make my insides melt. "Thank you."

I plan to say the words and push him away, and put some space between us, but I can't move. The way he watches me with such devotion and desire pins me in place. My pulse pounds faster and my skin prickles. My stomach swishes and flutters as the butterflies explode within me.

Nate doesn't touch me, but as he steps closer, dropping his arms from the tight fold across his chest, our noses brush together. I suck in a ragged breath and freeze in place. Kissing him here would be incredibly stupid. We're in a classroom. A student could walk in and see us. We'd both be screwed.

I finally confess, "Carter knows."

Nate blinks rapidly and pulls away the tiniest amount. "About us?"

"Yes, and he threatened to tell the dean. I don't want you to lose your job." I don't want to be labeled a whore either. I don't want to have other people dictate what we do. I don't want to hurt you. My eyes must say the rest of my thoughts because Nate seems to know.

Instead of pulling away, he leans in closer, presses his forehead to mine. "Neither do I."

"Then why are you still standing here?" A smile tugs at my lips. "You're too close."

"Because I want to kiss you." His voice is deep and rough. His dark lashes lower around those cool blue eyes as he speaks. "I've been thinking about you, about feeling your body against mine, slick with sweat. I want to make you cry out. I want to feel you tremble in my hands. I want to make you feel so good you can't stop smiling."

"Nate…"

He watches me through lowered lashes, lingering. "Use me, Kerry. Take out all your worry and anguish on me. I want you."

He watches my lips for a moment and then sweeps a kiss across them, gentle and teasing. My body tenses and I know I should push him away, but I don't want to. His hands are on my face, as he pulls my lips to his and the kiss deepens. His tongue is in my mouth and I don't want to stop. I feel his hard length pressing against my hip and visions of our naked tangled bodies flash behind my eyes.

Passion overtakes us and the kiss becomes frantic and heated. His hands are in my hair, tugging at the ponytail as he crushes his body against mine. The paintbrushes that are stuck in my hair fall to the floor. I nearly fall back into the painting, so Nate spins us around to the far wall and sets me down on the windowsill. He lunges to the side and swipes at the lights, dousing us with darkness.

I'm giddy when I realize what he wants to do. "We can't do that here."

Nate pushes my thighs apart and the fabric of my skirt offers plenty of room. He steps in between my legs so his hips are directly in front of mine. "We can do anything you want."

An image of the two of us, naked, and covered in paint while rolling across a canvas comes to mind. I push the thought away. This is crazy enough. That would be totally insane. His lips are on mine and he kisses me sweetly. "Tell me what you want, Kerry."

I sit there for a moment with Nate between my legs. He's leaning in, close to my face. There's a pale white light shining through the windows from the streetlamp outside. It spills across his face and dusts his dark hair with patches of white. "I want you, but—"

That's enough. Whatever self-restraint Nate had is gone. His mouth crushes against mine and I'm lost in a kiss so hot it makes the spot between my legs pulse. When he pulls away, I gasp for air and say his name softly. His lips are on my neck as his hands push my skirt past my hips. I hear his zipper and know there's only the thin fabric of my panties between us. He pulls my bottom to the edge of the counter and then positions himself just below me.

Looking into my eyes, he growls, "Fuck me, Kerry."

I gasp when I feel him push into me with no forewarning, no careful fingers. Suddenly he's there, filling me, hard and hot. I dig my nails into his neck and bite my lip to keep quiet. His hips press against mine and I take him deeper as he palms my ass, crushing me to him. I spread my thighs wider and latch my ankles around his hips.

He watches my eyes as he rocks into me, pushing in deep and then pulling out. The movement repeats and I can't keep my eyes on him. My head tips back and my mouth opens into an O. My ponytail dangles down my back as I clutch his shoulders and rock with him.

Nate breathes hard against my ear, pressing his cheek to mine, as he takes me harder and faster. The rhythmic movements become frantic until I'm wound so tightly that I nearly shatter. I buck wildly against his hips as I find my release and then still.

Hanging onto his shoulders, I open my eyes. "You weren't supposed to do that."

Nate's voice is rich and rumbles when he speaks. "No one tells me who I can fuck. If you want me, take me. If you don't, then leave."

That was a weird answer. I respond carefully. "It's not that simple."

"Yes, it is," he's watching my face now. He's still hard inside of me and presses his hips forward. I gasp and dig my nails into his shoulders. "Do you want this?" I nod slowly. "Say it, I need to hear you say it."

"I want you, Nate. I just don't want—"

He pulls away and I gasp with the sudden movement. He turns me around and commands, "Bend over."

I hesitate. "Someone will find us here. Nate—"

"No one is here at midnight. Kerry, it's just us." He positions himself behind me and presses me down over the counter so my ass is right in front of him. "Tell me you want it." He waits for me to say it, to agree with him before doing anything.

"Of course I want you. Nate, being with you is one of the best—" my words die in my mouth as he pushes into me. His thick shaft presses into my hot core and I gasp as I clutch the counter.

"Stop thinking. Let yourself feel and let go, Kerry."

I lay there as he fucks me senseless. I like the feel of him inside me without the condom and get lost in the sensations. We move from the window to a desk, changing positions. Although it's dark, I know he's watching me with every thrust of his hips, devouring the look on my face. It's incredibly sexy. I know he's completely here now, with me. There's nothing else in his mind, no one else breaks through. Not for either of us. I'm not comparing him to Matt anymore, or thinking about anything except how he makes me feel. Our bodies move together in silence until we're both spent and completely satisfied.

I smooth my skirt, run my hands over my hair, then bend over to pick up the paintbrushes that splattered on the floor. I have the happy, heaviness of being so thoroughly satisfied. The lazy grin lines my lips as I lean back against the counter.

Nate zips up and then glances at his phone. After he shoves it into his back pocket, he glances at me. His voice is flat when he says, "See you Monday."

I don't know what I expected, but when he turns to leave my heart drops. He doesn't offer to stay or even glance twice at me. I suppose this is what he felt like when he woke up alone last time.

I could linger back in the classroom and mope. I could act like it doesn't hurt, and fake it next time I see him. I could plan to fuck him again and make sure I leave first next time—that plan sounds awesome—but I don't want to wait. I rush after him, grabbing my bag, and following him down the hall.

"Hey," I'm suddenly next to him matching his long stride. "You're running off kind of quick."

He glances at me as we head down the stairs. He stops on the landing and turns to me. "Me? You were practically packing up your paintbrushes before I zipped up. I can take a hint, Kerry."

"What are you talking about? That wasn't a hint."

"Fine, call it whatever you want, but I get it. You just wanted a fuck and you don't want to get caught. We did that. It's over." He's cold and I don't understand why.

"Nate," I reach for his arm, but he shakes his head and rushes down the stairs.

He calls up to me without a glance in my direction. His feet hit the stairs in a quick rhythmic pattern, echoing in the darkness. "It's fine. We both did exactly what we said we'd do."

I lean over the banister and yell down at him. "Then why are you running away?"

He doesn't stop. Nate pushes through the doors and is gone.

I feel sick and lean my back to the wall, and slump down to the floor. I gather my knees into my chest and sit there for a while, replaying this evening's events. I don't understand why he bolted, and thinking about it isn't clarifying anything. What did I do wrong? Was this payback for bolting on him last week? Is he that petty? Or did I really hurt him by skipping out? I didn't mean to, but that doesn't seem to matter. The look in his eyes in the stairwell tonight wasn't something I want to remember. It was cold and calculating, like Ferro's soulless gaze.

There's nothing left to do but go home. I can't fix anything sitting here, and I don't want to cry anymore. When I stand, I don't realize that my foot is on the skirt, and the stitching pops as the hem tears.

CHAPTER 9

Sleep is evasive that night. Beth is mad at me, Carter turned evil, and Nate ran off like I doused his scorching body with ice water. I feel alone and it pains me, because I don't see how I could have prevented any of it. My actions weren't perfect, but I don't think they should have gotten me here. I frown and roll out of bed.

Chelsey is preening in front the mirror on her side of the room. She's been uncharacteristically silent since Matt and Mom were here. She fusses with her curling iron, trying to make her pin straight blonde locks fall in spirals. She hisses when the curl doesn't lay right and then glares at me. "What are you looking at, Bacon?"

I don't bother replying. She found the source of the stink under her bed and promised repayment tenfold for that little stunt. There's yet to be any move on her part. It makes me leery to sleep in the same room as her. If she ever got together with Carter, I'd be screwed.

I pad past her, go down the hall and shower. I take my time, hoping Chelsey will be gone when I get back to the room. When I pass a rumpled Beth in the hallway, she stares past me acting as if I didn't exist.

I roll my eyes without meaning to, and she sees it. Beth whirls around on me, towel over one arm, bath caddy in the other, and her body wrapped in a tight terrycloth robe. "Do you think it's funny? Do you think I'm a joke, and that none of this matters to me?"

I'm wearing a robe and have my damp towel in one hand and my bath bucket in the other. It's filled with shampoo, soap, razor, and shaving cream. I tossed my shower shoes in there too. It's not pretty like most of the girl's caddies with a cute pattern or pretty handle. I literally have a bucket from Wal-Mart. It cost a dollar instead of ten. Beth's caddy is designer, like her robe, towel, and shampoo. Maybe we're too different and this wouldn't have worked. Maybe I'm supposed to be a loner.

Either way, I need to diffuse this and get to my meeting before Ferro comes looking for me. As it is, I'm running late. "Beth, I don't want to fight with you. I'm sorry. I'll keep saying it until you accept my apology."

"That's never going to happen."

"Then there's nothing else I can do. I screwed up. You forgive me or you don't." I start to walk away and hear Beth make an aggravated sound in the back of her throat.

She growls at my back, "Do you know how hard it's been for me? Not just my family and my brothers, but everyone talks about Josh and what he did. Do you know what that's like? Loving someone who screwed up so royally?"

Turning, I look her in the eyes. "Yes, I do." My mother's face is vivid in my mind. It's not the same kind of mistake, but it damned our relationship and I can't fathom how to fix it. Apologies won't work, so I'm frozen, waiting for something to happen that forces forgiveness. Until then, I can't think about it without feeling sick.

"This is different. You're not a pariah because of your family. The only reason you were friends with me was because I gave you cookies." She looks away, frowning.

"I'm not five years old, Beth. I could have Googled you. I could have looked you up on Facebook or Instagram. I didn't, and that was intentional. I wanted to know who you are now, and the same thing goes for your brothers. I admit that I didn't like Josh at first. He was hot and cold, mean and sweet. I understand why he's so bipolar now—he doesn't trust himself anymore. I get that, and I don't blame you for something he did. You're not him."

"You kissed him. He told me. And I warned both of you, more than once. No, I begged you, I asked you to keep your distance. You didn't. I had my reasons and you didn't listen. What am I supposed to do with that?" She watches me with those large green eyes, pleading for an answer that I don't have. If I knew how to forgive someone for a massive betrayal, I would tell her. I'd take my own advice and patch things up with my mother, but I haven't a clue.

"I don't know." My voice is weak, ashamed that I hurt her so badly.

"All of this is tangled up for me. I don't want my friends hurt and I sure as hell don't want Josh—" her voice stops suddenly and she shakes her head.

We both watch each other for a moment, and when no more words are said, Beth walks away. It pains me that I can't make it better, that there seems to be no action that will win back her trust. I shove the thought aside and make my way to my room.

When I push through my door I can't believe what I see. The windows are open and my side of the room is empty. The bedding is stripped, my books are gone, and my closet is bare. The notes and papers that were on my white board are missing and the hastily scrawled messages have been erased. Meanwhile, Chelsey's side of the room is pristine with everything perfectly in place.

I set down my bath bucket and rush to the window. Leaning on the sill, I look out into the grassy area below. It connects to the back parking lot. My clothes are scattered below, laying on the ground and hanging from trees while the papers fly away with the Texas wind. My textbooks, alarm clock, and bedding are blowing into the parking lot. A few students are gathered on the grass below and at the center is a blonde woman with long curls. Her laughter flutters up and I'm livid.

I have to be at a meeting, I'm already late, and my suit—along with everything I own—has been scattered to the wind. I could race down the stairs and beat the crap out of Chelsey, but we'll both get suspended. Or she'll be gone before I get down there.

Screw it. I'm sick of people messing with me. Robe tied tight, I'm out the window and on the ledge. I pad barefoot toward the fire escape and rush down the steps. When I'm on the second floor, I twist and hurl myself off the ledge and land in the grass like a deranged ninja.

Screaming wildly, I rush at my roommate. Until then, she was laughing and pointing up at me. Now, she has a horrified look on her face. Her eyes are wide and she turns to run, but her pack of idiots doesn't part. She's trapped and I rush at her, slamming into her, and knocking her to the ground.

People gather around and start chanting *fight, fight, fight.* Chelsey's friends make bacon jokes and jeer at me as I grab their friend by the hair, roll her over, and push her face into the dirt.

"Apologize!" I scream as I make her eat grass.

Chelsey spits and squeals, wiggling beneath me, trying to break free. "No! Get off me, you pig!"

She shrills again when I shove her face into the lawn. "Say you're sorry!"

I let her up for air and give her a chance to say it. Her pink lips snarl and she spits out the words, "I'll never say I'm sorry to someone like you, you cheap slut!"

I'm not doing this all day. If she wants to be the center of attention, then I'm granting her wish. Without a word, I yank the tie off my robe and it falls open. A few guys whistle and cheer. I'm aware of flashes going off, which means there will be pictures of me sitting with an open robe on top of my roommate with her pristine face in the grass, but I don't care.

Tugging her arms behind her back, I loop the fabric around her wrists and then grab her ankles, bending her knees and twisting the belt around quickly. I knot it off, and stand. Closing my robe with my hands, I walk away leaving Chelsey tied up, face-first in the dirt.

A guy behind me bellows, "Holy shit! Yankee Chick hog-tied her!"

The comment spreads through the crowd like a wave and as I storm away. More students are rushing over, phones out, with flashes flaring as they take pictures. Rushing at a grouping of shrubs, I pluck my suit from the branches and scurry inside as more students race out. Someone claps me on the back, thanking me for putting that bitch in her place. When I get to my hall, my resident advisor smiles at me as she passes by me.

Was Chelsey horrible to everyone? I thought she was only picking on me.

When I'm in our room again, I shut the door and look out the window. She's still lying there, screaming. No one helps her. A sinking feeling slithers across my stomach and I feel bad for her. Even her friends post her red face and hogtied hands and feet on Facebook rather than helping her up.

I ditch the robe and pull on the suit. I have no stockings and no bra. I grab an extra pair of undies from my gym bag and pull them on. Meeting Ferro with no bra is insane. He's going to think I want him or something worse. I button the suit jacket and look down at my figure. It's harder to tell that I'm swinging free.

I whip my hair into a quick bun and look out the window for my shoes. They're by the parking lot. I pad back down the stairs, rush past Beth who watches me with sad eyes, and shove through the doors. As I slip on the second shoe, I glance back into the square. Chelsey is still there. Campus police didn't show up. What the hell? They should have stopped this by now.

I could turn and walk away. She deserved everything she got, but the prolonged humiliation and heckling from the wild crowd around her pisses me off. Someone should have helped her up by now. I can't believe there's not one Good Samaritan in the lot of them.

"Damn it," I growl and march across the lawn. I shove my pointy elbows into the crowd, forcing my way to the center. When I get there I see Chelsey crying, still lying on her stomach, but now she's covered in marker.

Someone wrote on her. Across her forehead it says BITCH. Along her cheek, smeared by tears, is the word WHORE. She whips her face the other way and the letters C.U.N.T. are on her other cheek.

Oh. My. God. Chelsey is screaming as tears run down her face. Grass and dirt stick to her once perfect skin, obscuring the words. A fat permanent marker lies next to her on the grass. Students are shouting demands to roll her over and keep writing on her legs, suggesting more insults to brand her with.

I bellow at them, red-faced, "WHAT THE HELL IS WRONG WITH YOU?"

I don't wait for a reply. They've turned into a mob of crazy people. I swoop in, lifting my batshit crazy roommate, and carrying her like a baby in my arms. Holy crap, she's heavy. I need to do more pushups. I run-walk across the lawn, making a beeline for my bus at the edge of the parking lot. I'm turning into a sweaty mess and my suit is sticking to my body. The parking lot is so close. I think about putting her down and untying her once there's enough distance between the crowd and Chelsey, but after a few moments some of the guys in the crowd follow me.

"Come back here, we weren't done yet," one guy with dark hair and really broad shoulders calls out behind me. They walk slowly and I feel frantic, like I'm being chased by zombies on steroids.

When my feet hit asphalt I know I can get on the bus before they reach me. Thank God they don't decide to run. I round the front of the bus and grunt up the stairs, hoisting Chelsey higher, and banging my knee into her butt by accident. My center of gravity shifts and I trip.

Chelsey falls on the floor and cries out, "You stupid bitch! You did this to me and now you're kidnapping me! I'm going to sue your ass off and make you so poor you'll have to hang your toilet paper up to dry!"

"Shut up, Chelsey. I'm trying to save your pampered ass." I hurry and shove the handle that closes the doors. They shut and I crawl up into the driver's seat, grabbing the keys from the floor and then forcing them into the ignition and turn over the engine.

A group of guys rushes the bus and one of them manages to pry open the door. They're acting insane—like they want to beat the crap out both of us. I can't get the bus into gear and drive away with them inside. I don't know what to do. I don't have pepper spray on me. It's in my purse. I'm lucky I left the keys in the bus. No one stole it as hoped for, but we can get away if I can keep these guys from storming my bus.

Three of them shove up the stairs at the same time, two in front and one in back. They make it to the second step when the wild hissing starts.

It's coming from the seat above Chelsey's head. Pita, that rabid fur ball, is perched on top of the seat. He swats an inky paw at them as spittle flies from his black lips.

The bus lurches to life and the startled men fall backward. They land on the pavement in the parking lot in a pile. I don't stop. I keep driving until we're off school property.

When I stop at the traffic light, still shaking, Kevin the bike cop starts yelling in through the open door. "Pull over!"

I glance at him and then back at Chelsey who's cursing and crying in the aisle. She got quieter when the raccoon decided to sit on her hair. Pita is picking foliage from it and sniffing each piece like he might want to eat it.

I glance at Kevin and put the bus in park. This looks really bad, but I could use his assistance. Maybe he won't report me. At this point, I expect Chelsey to set me on fire and take everything I own. I'm screwed either way.

I sigh at him. "I am pulled over. Come up here. I need your help."

Kevin blinks, surprise washing across his face. I rush down the aisle, which makes Pita rush back to his hiding spot at the back of the bus. I untie Chelsey, bracing for her to claw my face off when I pull her up, but instead she falls apart in my arms. Sobs shake her body and she hugs me tightly.

When Kevin walks up the stairs, he sees her and freezes. The guy is one hundred percent dork with shortly cropped hair and ill-fitting uniform. He's the kind of guy that would never approach Chelsey, but today he does. He carefully asks, "Are you all right?"

Chelsey looks up at him and bawls louder.

I pry her off of me and loop her arms around Kevin's neck. "Please take her home. Wash the marker off her face and give her something to eat."

He swears, muttering, pulling back her long blonde locks to see what's written on her skin. "Is that permanent?"

"I think so. There's acetone in our room." He stares at me like I'm speaking Greek. "It's nail polish remover. It'll strip off anything."

He nods. "Who did this to her? Did you get any names?"

I'm about to say I did it, but Chelsey lifts her face from his shoulder. Bottom lip quivering, she glances at me. "I didn't see them and I don't want to file a report. Just please take me home."

We lock eyes for a moment and it's like she understands how her jeers had repercussions, that it wasn't simply an unkind word from her lips on those days she spewed her venom my way. It was the on-lookers who jumped in and made it worse.

"Thank you." Her words are shocking, soft, but firm.

Kevin takes her down the stairs, cooing kind words to her as they go. Chelsey lets him help and doesn't say another word.

I sit there stunned for a moment and catch a chill. "Oh my God. Hell froze over."

CHAPTER 10

I pull up in front of the lawyer's office where I met Ferro the first time. It's early and the parking lot is empty. I head inside and wander down the hallway until I'm standing in front of the door to the office. I swallow hard and shove my way inside.

I've thought about what kind of favor he might ask me for and all sorts of things crossed my mind from something illegal to sexual favors. I hope I'm not his type. My boobs aren't plastic and I'm a brunette. As far as I can tell, Ferro likes busty blondes.

I feel weary. When I push through the doors, I put on my poker face. I have to bullshit my way through this. When I enter, I scan the room.

Ferro is standing in front of the floor to ceiling wall of windows with a cigar in his hand.

He turns and those steely gray eyes meet mine, sending a chill down my spine. "Miss Hill."

"Mr. Ferro." I walk over to the leather chairs we sat in last time, but I don't sit down. I stand there in my rumpled suit with my messy bun and hot face. I worked up a sweat carrying Chelsey. I couldn't have carried her at all if she actually ate anything. I'm hot and sweaty, and it shows.

His gaze sweeps over me. "Do you always work out in your suit?"

"Yes." I spit out the word without emotion, adding, "I sleep in it too, hence the wrinkles."

"It's shocking that you don't have a criminal record. You're young, desperate, and financially unstable."

I don't react to his insult. Instead, I add, "You forgot emotionally deprived."

"Yes, thank you for reminding me." Ferro sucks on his cigar and then slowly lets out a long slit of smoke from between his lips. It's disgusting. Everything from the smell to the lingering smoke nauseates me.

"What do you want?" Asking the question gives him the upper hand, but he already has it. There's no point in lingering today.

"It's simple, Miss Hill. You have a connection that I need in order to progress my plans. I've been preparing for this for nearly three decades, and despite one minor transgression, I've managed to keep things moving forward." The way he says 'minor transgression' makes the hairs on the back of my neck stand on end.

"What are you talking about?"

"Oil, black gold. People said Texas was run dry, that there was no way to get at the massive amount of wealth locked beneath layers of stone, but I persisted. I purchased the land and waited. We refined and experimented with the best means to pull the oil from the earth and after decades of waiting, it's finally time to reap the rewards."

"What do you need me for?"

Ferro turns away and takes another long pull on his cigar. When he finally answers, he only says one word. "Nathan."

"What about him?"

"Your little stunt got him back his house, but he can't keep it. I thought I'd buy him out, pay him handsomely for the property, and he'd vacate. It should have been a non-issue, a minor annoyance. Every other homeowner in that neighborhood sold out, save one. I've offered him more than a fair amount, and he still refuses to leave."

"So, what do you want me to do?"

Ferro slowly turns, letting the sun illuminate his lean figure on one side, while hiding his face in harsh shadows. "Make him sell."

I make a sound of protest and swat a hand at him. "Why do you think he'll listen to me?"

Ferro steps closer, gets in my face, and hisses, "Don't make the mistake of thinking that I need this favor to move forward, Miss Hill. I do not. This is your mess, your complication. I'm simply giving you the chance to clean it up, before I do."

The way he says it, cold, detached and ruthless sends a sheet of ice over my skin. His handsome features become hard lines and deadly shadows. His threat makes me shiver. I step away without meaning to, which results in Ferro stepping closer. "Three days. You have three days to convince Nathan Smith to move or I'll take matters in a direction he will not like."

COMING SOON:

SECRETS & LIES 7

Make sure you don't miss it! Text HMWARD (one word) to 24587 to receive a text reminder on release day.

***

Turn the page to enjoy a free excerpt of

STRIPPED 2:
A FERRO FAMILY NOVEL

CHAPTER 1: CASSIE

With Jon's coat wrapped around my shoulders and the blanket draped over my hips, I watch the two women on stage. Their laughter rings true, and I can't help feeling envious. Their lives must be so much easier than mine. I haven't laughed myself sick for a very long time. A combination of tears and terror ward off any moments of pure bliss.

I feel Jon's gaze on the side of my face. He leans close so we're nearly cheek-to-cheek and whispers, "As far as I know, they both have a bag of demonic cats living in their brains. That chick," he nods at Sidney, "confronted my mother."

My jaw drops and I stare at him, gaping. "No." The word is drawn out, and my unspoken question hangs in the air—who has the balls to challenge Constance Ferro?

"Yes. That one," he points to Avery, "she's still fighting the tide, but refuses to go under."

"How do you know that?"

He shrugs. "I sense it." I suspect there's a story behind his comments, but Jon dodges further discussion by joining Trystan by the stage.

Trystan Scott—blue-eyed heartthrob, sex on a stick, and all around ladies man—pushes back into the dark leather chair, worry pinching the tanned skin between his eyebrows. Dark hair falls into his eyes as he claws the arm of his seat, backing away from the crazy chick making herself at home in his lap.

Sidney and Avery stand arm in arm in mirrored poses, their opposite hands on their hips. Avery calls out, "Hey, little bro Ferro." She laughs and says to Sidney, "He's not very little is he?"

Sidney shakes her head and giggles. "I've heard nothing about him is little."

Peter, who had been standing quietly behind me, is suddenly across the room and marching up the steps. "Hey!"

Sidney smiles at him as he crosses the stage and wraps her arms around his waist. "Girls like to talk, and it's hard to avoid hearing rumors since people ask me way too frequently about you."

Peter's eyes turn into beach balls, and he nearly chokes. "Excuse me? Where do people ask you these things?"

She shrugs, ticking off a list on her fingers. "At the market, at school, in the ladies room." She looks over at Avery. "Do they bug you about Sean?"

"They think I'm a hooker, so I'm invisible." Avery picks at a spot of glitter on her arm. "Besides, my profession doesn't exactly make me a credible source. Who cares if Sean's call girl said he's huge?"

Everyone stops and gawks at her. Bryan stops teasing Trystan to give his full attention to Avery. "He hired you?"

Stunned faces snap to hers, but Avery's expression remains placid as if she's accepted it and moved on. In the echoing silence, a needle could drop and sound like a grenade.

Jon practically growls, "I don't know why anyone is shocked. We are talking about Sean." He seems pissed, and shoots a quick glance at me from the corner of his eye, then moves across the room to sit by Trystan.

There's a sinking feeling in the pit of my stomach. Based on the facial expressions of the people here with me, I'd guess it's contagious— we all feel it.

I keep my eyes down, but I hate that Jon said it. I hate the way no one tries to protect her. Strength on the outside is just that—outside. It doesn't keep the world from trampling your heart.

I find my voice, "She's more than that, you know." The words spill out, and once I start I can't stop. I jump up, dropping the jacket and blanket behind me. I pad toward him, standing there covered in glitter, my corset hoisting my breasts to my throat and my thong revealing my entire backside.

Jon realizes how it sounded and attempts to correct, but he's already flown that thought into a mountainside. "I know, but—"

"No little girl says, 'I want to be a stripper when I grow up.' Not one of us would sell sex if there'd been another way to survive. Every single woman who works here has the same story— fucked up life, no money, and no hope. Don't you dare damn her for it! If you do, you're damning me, too, and I refuse to accept your pity, or whatever the hell this is." I'm in his face, an inch from his nose, breathing hard. It looks like I'm going to pop out of my corset every time I breathe. Mounds of flesh swell well above the low neckline, glittering like twin disco balls.

I expect him to look at me, but he doesn't. Jon presses his lips together, letting his silence build between us while the others stare in shock. When his blue gaze lifts to meet mine, he tips his head to the side. No trace of a smile softens his lips. Nothing subdues his sharp look. "You don't know Sean. He'd show up with a corpse if it suited him."

Something inside me snaps. I straighten, laughing bitterly. "You're an asshole."

"No, I'm not. I'm just saying—"

"Shut up, man. She hears exactly what you're saying." Trystan peers around the girl in his lap, forgetting his own awkward situation for the moment. The girl sits perfectly still, but I can see her thoughts running wild behind her eyes.

Jon growls, "No, she doesn't. This isn't about any of you. It's about my brother and me." There's obviously a huge rift between Jon and Sean, but he's poking a bear with Pixy Stix. What does he think is going to happen?

"It might also be about your apparent distaste for working girls." Avery folds her arms over her chest and juts one hip to the side, glaring at him. "So, Little Ferro, spill it. Did your first hooker mistreat you? Or was it one of your strippers?"

Jon's body tenses and he sits so still he might explode. It's the moment of utter silence before a bomb detonates and blasts everything around it to bits. One of his fingers presses into the chair, and I see something flash across his face. It's raw, a wound that's still weeping.

He's quiet for a moment, swallows hard, then stands and walks into the office. The door closes soundlessly behind him. Something happened to him. I'm sure of that. Someone hurt him badly.

Apparently Avery senses it too because she slips off the edge of the stage and rushes toward me. "I'm sorry. I didn't know."

I glance at the closed door and then back to her pale face. "Neither did I. I'm not sure any of us did."

CHAPTER 2: JON

I feel like a fucking idiot walking away to hide in the office. I'm not a kid anymore. This shit shouldn't bother me, but it's always lurking—ready to rear its fuck-ugly face when I least expect it. Of course they all think I had hookers and strippers. I'm not a priest. I'm a Ferro. I live up to my reputation and then some. But that's not what made me back down. I know I don't see things accurately at times. I know my past taints my vision, clouds it, and makes me respond in the worst possible ways.

I sit down at the desk and stare at the packet of papers. I wonder if I'm reacting to Sean or my past. How can I protect Cass when I can't even deal with this?

There's a knock on my door, and before I can answer, Avery steps inside.

"Hey," she says, "I didn't mean to do that." She's standing there, her long brown hair sweeping over her shoulders and a somber expression on her face. She steps around the door, pushing it shut behind her with the heel of her foot. No shoes.

"You didn't do anything." I'm not telling her shit. She'll report back to Sean, and I don't want him involved in this. His chance to intercede is long gone.

I shuffle through the stack of papers on the desk, ignoring Sean's envelope. I'll look at it when she leaves.

"Maybe not, but it seemed like I found a sore spot and ripped it wide open."

I act like it doesn't matter. I'm not telling her shit. "I misspoke. Cassie is hurting. It was reasonable to assume I insulted all of you."

Avery stops in front of my desk, turns to a ninety-degree angle from me, and rests her denim-clad hip against it. She folds her arms loosely across her chest. "We're all hurting."

I glance up at her. Is that a hint? Is something going on with my brother? "Sean included?"

Her eyes dart to the side. She pushes off the desk and looks at a picture of the club on the wall. All the dancers are standing with the bouncers and the former owner, posing as if it were a yearbook picture. "You don't know him anymore, do you?"

"There's nothing about him that's worth knowing." I sound like a cold motherfucker, like I don't give a shit about my brother, but the tightening sensation in my chest tells me otherwise. The growing unease in my stomach, the way it twists like it's filled with shards of glass, reminds me of something I don't want to admit. I suppress it with one swift blow, forcing my emotions back down where they belong. "Maybe you don't know, so I'll tell you the drive-by version. Sean thinks I'm a piece of shit stuck to his shoe. No one willingly walks through shit, Avery. He's here to save his ass. It has nothing to do with me."

"You don't know him."

I appreciate the audacity of this woman. This is the first conversation we've had, beyond initial pleasantries, and she's picking a fight? I lean back in my chair and look at her. She's smart. I'd bet anything that she's scanning that picture for Cassie's face. It's not there. Cass always dodges pictures, probably because of her ex.

I roll my eyes and sit up quickly, reshuffling papers that don't need it. "I don't want to know him. There's nothing there worth saving, no way we'll ever be anything but blood. I don't give a shit what he does or if someone puts a bullet in his head. Actually, I've been waiting for it to happen. Between his past and the shitstorm in the press, it's only a matter of time. I wouldn't get too attached, Avery." It's a dick thing to say, but this conversation is over.

She takes the hint and heads to the door. Her hand rests on the knob for a second then she looks over her shoulder at me. "Too late. I'm already attached." She smiles sadly, watching me until I meet her eyes. "And no matter what you think, Sean cares about you. I see it in his eyes. I hear it in his voice when he talks about you. Think what you want, but take it from someone who knows what it's like to be utterly alone—Sean's here out of more than loyalty. You're more than blood to him. I'll see you around." She walks through the door without waiting for a reply.

Continue reading STRIPPED 2 now!

COMING SEPTEMBER 2016

After 3 years of begging, you finally got it!

A DAMAGED WEDDING

Pre-order begins now. Tell your friends! Help make Peter and Sidney's wedding awesome!

MORE FERRO FAMILY BOOKS

JONATHAN FERRO
~STRIPPED~

******

TRYSTAN SCOTT
~BROKEN PROMISES~

******

NICK FERRO
~THE WEDDING CONTRACT~

*****

BRYAN FERRO
~THE PROPOSITION~

*****

SEAN FERRO
~THE ARRANGEMENT~

******

PETER FERRO GRANZ
~DAMAGED~

*****

MORE ROMANCE BY H.M. WARD

SCANDALOUS

SCANDALOUS 2

SECRETS

THE SECRET LIFE OF TRYSTAN SCOTT

DEMON KISSED

CHRISTMAS KISSES

SECOND CHANCES

And more.

To see a full book list, please visit:
www.HMWard.com/#!/BOOKS

CAN'T WAIT FOR *H.M. WARD'S NEXT STEAMY BOOK?*

★ ★ ★ ★ ★

Let her know by leaving stars and telling her
what you liked about
SECRETS & LIES 6
in a review!

ABOUT THE AUTHOR
H.M. WARD

New York Times bestselling author HM Ward
continues to reign as the queen of independent
publishing. She is swiftly approaching 13 MILLION
copies sold, placing her among the literary titans.
Articles pertaining to Ward's success have appeared in
The New York Times, USA Today, and Forbes to name
a few. This native New Yorker resides in Texas with her
family, where she enjoys working on her next book.

You can interact with this bestselling author at:
Twitter: @HMWard
Facebook: AuthorHMWard
Webpage: www.hmward.com